Finding a Friend

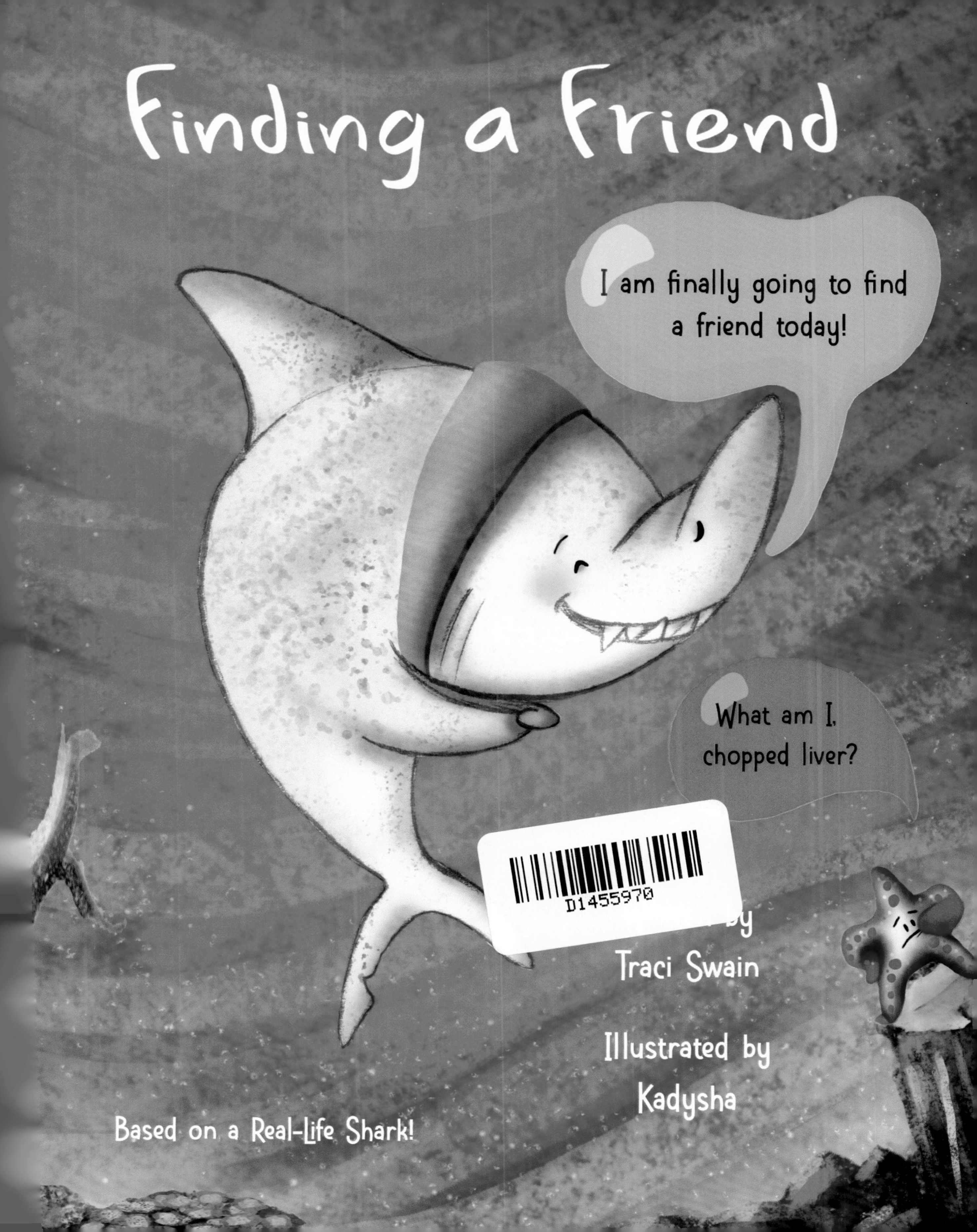

by
Traci Swain

Illustrated by
Kadysha

Based on a Real-Life Shark!

Dedicated to my mom, Emma Swain.
I am eternally grateful for her unconditional love,
strength, and support.

Babe always follow your dream

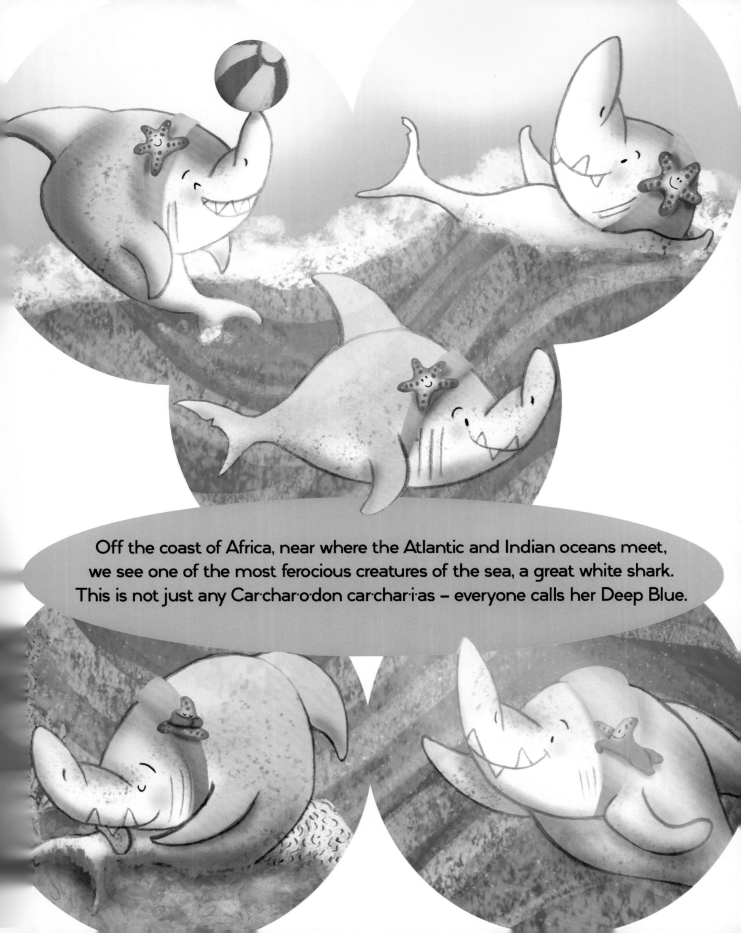

Off the coast of Africa, near where the Atlantic and Indian oceans meet,
we see one of the most ferocious creatures of the sea, a great white shark.
This is not just any Car·char·o·don car·char·i·as – everyone calls her Deep Blue.

And then what happened?

Well, that's pretty much the end of my story.
Anyhoo, when I woke up this morning,
you know what I decided?. . .

What?

That today is the perfect day to. . .

...FIND A FRIEND!

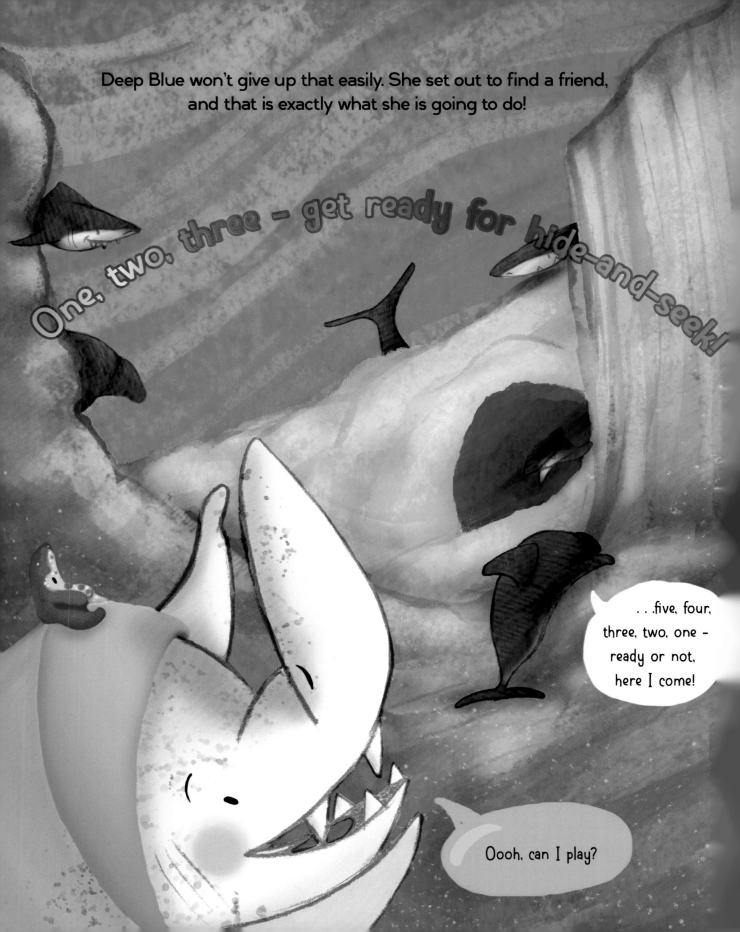

Deep Blue won't give up that easily. She set out to find a friend, and that is exactly what she is going to do!

One, two, three – get ready for hide-and-seek!

. . .five, four, three, two, one – ready or not, here I come!

Oooh, can I play?

Any self-respecting shark knows that when meeting someone new you should introduce yourself.

Where are our manners? Allow us to introduce ourselves. My name is Deep Blue, and this is Cushy.

Cushy?

Short for Panamic cushion star. I'm a Pen·ta·cer·as·ter cu·min·gi. What's your scientific name?

I'm just Peter Penguin.

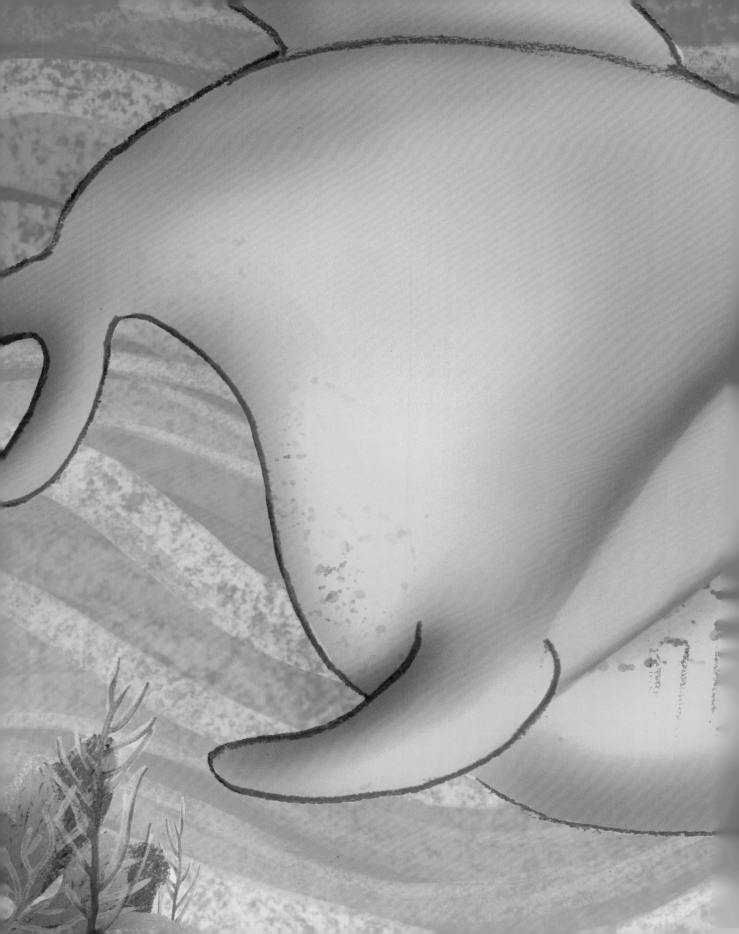

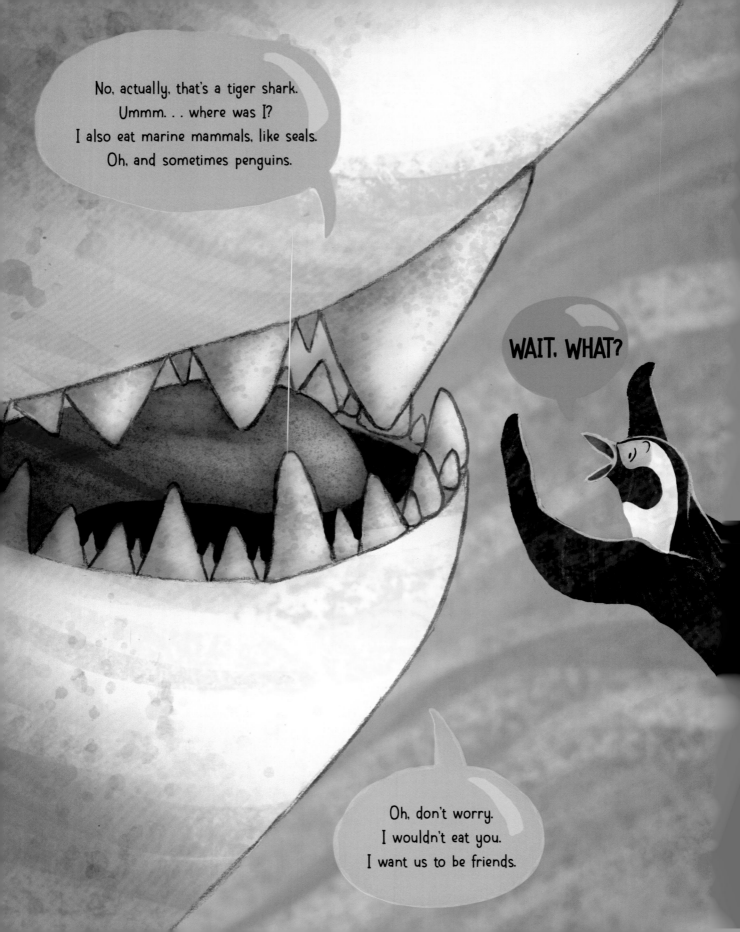

Oh, and I can do this cool thing called breaching.
Whales can do it too, but I'm really good at it.
I jump out of the water and then twist to catch my prey!
It's awesome! Wanna see?

Ummm. . . Well,
I think we have to go.

You know, sometimes your friends are right in front of your face - or on your headband.
You are absolutely right. Cushy, you're my very best friend.
Do you mean it?
Yes! And how lucky am I to have found a friend like you?

Fun Facts

DEEP BLUE

Type of Shark: Great White

Scientific Name: Carcharodon carcharias

This great white shark can travel at a speed of up to 16 mph. She is an apex predator with triangular teeth that are as sharp as blades and can grow up to 3 inches long. She loves to eat, travel, and make new friends.

Weight: 5,000 lb

Length: 20 ft.

PEPPER & PETER

Type of Penguin: African P

Scientific Name: Spheniscus de

These flightless seabirds are found or southwestern coast of South Africa. T pink patches of skin above their eyes distinguish them from other penguin species. Pepper loves to swim and Peter loves long walks on the beach.

Length: 24 & 26 in.

Weight 5 & 6

CUSHY

Type of Starfish: Panamic Cushion Star

Scientific Name: Pentaceraster cumingi

Cushy has an incredible regenerative power: when attacked, she can grow back new arms. She is an omnivore and feeds on things like worms and seagrass. Her favorite hobbies are reading and learning new things.

Weight: 9 lb

Length: 12 ft.

Glossary

1. *Carcharodon carcharias* (Car·char·o·don car·char·i·as): The great white shark is a predator with a body shaped like a torpedo. These sharks can grow to about 20 feet, and some scientists think they might be descendants of the massive prehistoric shark called megalodon.

2. *Arctocephalus pusillus* (Arc·to·ceph·a·lus pu·sil·lus): The brown fur seal, sometimes known as the South African fur seal, is the largest of its kind. They can grow as long as 7 feet and weigh over 600 pounds. They get their name because they have two layers of fur on their body.

3. *Pentaceraster cumingi* (Pen·ta·cer·as·ter cu·min·gi): This starfish can be found from northern Peru to as far north as the Gulf of California. They can grow up to 12 inches wide.

4. *Mammal* : A warm-blooded animal. The females have glands that allow them to produce milk for their babies. All mammals have either hair or fur.

Some examples are humans, elephants, and whales.
5. *Tiger shark:* A shark with dark stripes down its body. They can grow to over 16 feet long. They will eat pretty much anything. That is why we call them "garbage eaters." Its scientific name is *Galeocerdo cuvier* (Ga·le·o·cer·do cu·vier).

6. *Spheniscus demersus* (Sphe·nis·cus de·mer·sus): The African penguin is one of the smaller of the groups of penguins. They are between 24 and 28 inches tall and can weigh up to a little over 7 pounds. The best part – they don't have any teeth.

7. *Pescatarian* (Pes·ca·tar·i·an): Those who only eat fish or seafood. They never eat meat.

8. *Breaching* : When an animal jumps out of the water (headfirst) and then lands with a loud splash.

Dear Reader,

I was extremely lucky when it came to friends.
My first friend became my best friend. Dalia and I met when I was eight
and she was nine, and we are still close to this day.

My mother always said, "You choose your friends,
don't let your friends choose you." I offer that advice to you today.
Be selective in those with whom you share your time.

A true friend is a person who respects and cares for you.
Someone who listens and understands what you might be going through.
Someone to laugh with, and someone who stays around to help when things
are not feeling so great. But don't forget, you have to be a good friend
to them too! All of the qualities you admire in them
you can find in yourself as well.

I am so excited at the prospect of you finding a friend.
In the meantime, enjoy spending time with the best friend
you'll ever have - YOU!

Your friend, Traci

Thank you to my Favorite Group of Advisers
Ali, Ann Marie and Tonya

Traci is lucky to have you!

Library of Congress Control Number: 2021900581
Library of Congress Cataloging-in-Publication Data
available upon request

International
Standard
Book Number

ISBN
978-1-7364802-2-9 (Hardcover)
978-1-7364802-0-5 (Paperback)
978-1-7364802-1-2 (e-book)

And remember,
it's important to be
a good friend.

Printed in the U.S.A.
10 9 8 7 6 5 4 3 2 1

The illustrations were created with digital drawings.